The Tortoise and the Hare

Is speed important in a race?

www.av2books.com

Go to **www.av2books.com**, and enter this book's unique code.

BOOK CODE

Y122523

AV² by Weigl brings you media enhanced books that support active learning.

Published by AV² by Weigl
350 5th Avenue, 59th Floor New York, NY 10118

Copyright ©2013 AV² by Weigl
Copyright ©2010 by Kyowon Co., Ltd.

Library of Congress Cataloging-in-Publication Data

The tortoise and the hare.
    p. cm. -- (Aesop's fables by AV2)
 Summary: The familiar Aesop fable is performed by a troupe of animal actors.
 ISBN 978-1-61913-103-3
 [1. Fables. 2. Folklore.] I. Aesop.
 PZ8.2.T59 2012
 398.2--dc23
 [E]
                                    2012018618

Printed in the United States in North Mankato, Minnesota
1 2 3 4 5 6 7 8 9 0 16 15 14 13 12

052012
WEP110612

FABLE SYNOPSIS

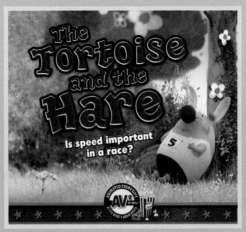

For thousands of years, parents and teachers have used memorable stories called fables to teach simple moral lessons to children.

In the Aesop's Fables by AV² series, classic fables are given a lighthearted twist. These familiar tales are performed by a troupe of animal players whose endearing personalities bring the stories to life.

In *The Tortoise and the Hare*, Aesop and his troupe teach their audience that hard work and determination will pay off in the end. Slow and steady wins the race!

This AV² media enhanced book comes alive with...

Animated Video
Watch a custom animated movie.

Try This!
Complete activities and hands on experiments.

Key Words
Study vocabulary and hands-on experiments.

Quiz
Test your knowledge.

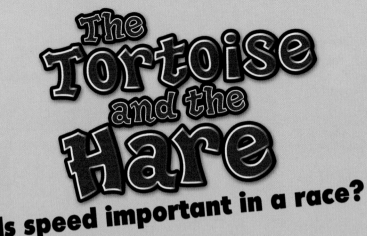

The Tortoise and the Hare

Is speed important in a race?

AV² Storytime Navigation

TRY THIS

KEY WORDS

Quiz

CLOSE

PLAY/PAUSE MOVIE

HOME

VIDEO LENGTH

VOLUME

INFO — TITLE INFORMATION

3

The Players

Aesop
I am the leader of Aesop's Theater, a screenwriter, and an actor.
I can be hot-tempered, but I am also soft and warm-hearted.

Libbit
I am an actor and a prop man.
I think I should have been a lion, but I was born a rabbit.

Presy
I am the manager of Aesop's Theater.
I am also the narrator of the plays.

4

Elvis
I like dance and music. I am artistic. I am very good at drawing.

Bogart
I am the strongest and the oldest pig. I always do whatever I want.

Audrey
I am a very good and caring pig. If someone cries, I cry with them. I never lie.

Milala
I think I am cute. I like to get attention from the other animals.

Goddard
I am very greedy. I like food.

5

The Story

One morning, Libbit and
Aesop were arguing.
"It's nonsense! The hare is
fast, and the tortoise is slow.
Why does the hare lose the race?" said Libbit.
"It teaches an important lesson!" said Aesop.
"I don't want to be in this play. A tortoise beats
a rabbit in a race? It's nonsense."
Libbit sulked.
"Elvis, you'll play the hare, and I'll play the
tortoise," announced Aesop.

Presy appeared on the stage.
"Aesop's Theater presents
The Tortoise and the Hare."
Presy waited, but the gong did
not sound.
Libbit did not want to ring it.
Aesop, dressed as a tortoise,
hit the gong instead.
The curtain rose.

One spring day, a hare met a tortoise in a field.

The hare said, "You must be a slow runner!"

"I'm not so slow! Shall we run a race?" asked the tortoise.

"Okay. Let's race to the top of the big hill."

The hare and the tortoise were ready to race.

"Ready... Set... Go!" said Goddard.

The hare took off when the whistle blew.

The tortoise started slowly.

"I am much faster!" the hare bragged.

The tortoise walked on and on.

Who would win the race?

Aesop was having trouble walking.

"My tortoise shell is so heavy!"

Libbit was glad to see Aesop having trouble.

"I made sure the tortoise shell would be heavy!"

Libbit said quietly to himself.

"How silly the tortoise is!

He is very slow, so I'll have time to rest."

The hare laid down in the shade and fell asleep.

The tortoise kept walking towards the finish line.

"Phew! This shell is so heavy, and it's so hot in here!"

The tortoise walked and walked.

The hare was still sleeping.

The tortoise passed the hare!

Suddenly, giant rocks fell in front of Aesop.

Libbit was trying to block his path.

He was still upset with Aesop.

"I'll make sure that the hare wins," said Libbit.

19

"Bang!"

A big rock hit Aesop's shell.

He fell over, but could not move

because the shell was too heavy.

Libbit ran to help Aesop.

"I'm sorry! I didn't mean to hit you!"

Libbit rolled Aesop onto

his feet and helped him

get to the top

of the hill.

21

The Shorties were holding a
flag at the end of the race.
Libbit and Aesop were near the finish line when Aesop
slipped and tumbled down the hill.
Libbit and the Shorties chased after him.
"Aesop, are you ok?" cried Libbit.

Aesop came to a stop at the
bottom of the hill.
Libbit ran into the Shorties,
and they all fell next to Aesop.
Aesop picked up the flag.
"I won!"
The tortoise won the race.

After the play, Libbit apologized to Aesop.

"I didn't mean to hurt you Aesop. I'm sorry!"

"That's ok, Libbit. Everybody liked the play."

"The audience thought you were acting," said Presy.

Libbit smiled. "I sure learned my lesson!"

Slow and steady wins the race.

What is a Story?

Players

Who is the story about? The characters, or players, are the people, animals, or objects that perform the story. Characters have personality traits that contribute to the story. Readers understand how a character fits into the story by what the character says and does, what others say about the character, and how others treat the character.

Setting

Where and when do the events take place? The setting of a story helps readers visualize where and when the story is taking place. These details help to suggest the mood or atmosphere of the story. A setting is usually presented briefly, but it explains whether the story is taking place in the past, present, or future and in a large or small area.

Plot

What happens in the story? The plot is a story's plan of action. Most plots follow a pattern. They begin with an introduction and progress to the rising action of events. The events lead to a climax, which is the most exciting moment in the story. The resolution is the falling action of events. This section ties up loose ends so that readers are not left with unanswered questions. The story ends with a conclusion that brings the events to a close.

Point of View

Who is telling the story? The story is normally told from the point of view of the narrator, or storyteller. The narrator can be a main character or a less important character in the story. He or she can also be someone who is not in the story but is observing the action. This observer may be impartial or someone who knows the thoughts and feelings of the characters. A story can also be told from different points of view.

Dialogue

What type of conversation occurs in the story? Conversation, or dialogue, helps to show what is happening. It also gives information about the characters. The reader can discover what kinds of people they are by the words they say and how they say them. Writers use dialogue to make stories more interesting. In dialogue, writers imitate the way real people speak, so it is written differently than the rest of the story.

Theme

What is the story's underlying meaning? The theme of a story is the topic, idea, or position that the story presents. It is often a general statement about life. Sometimes, the theme is stated clearly. Other times, it is suggested through hints.

The Tortoise and the Hare

Quiz

1 Who was in the race?

2 Who made the tortoise shell heavy?

3 What did Libbit push onto the path?

4 Who fell asleep?

5 Who won the race?

6 What lesson did Libbit learn?

Key Words

Research has shown that as much as 65 percent of all written material published in English is made up of 300 words. These 300 words cannot be taught using pictures or learned by sounding them out. They must be recognized by sight. This book contains 102 common sight words to help young readers improve their reading fluency and comprehension. This book also teaches young readers several important content words, such as proper nouns. These words are paired with pictures to aid in learning and improve understanding.

Page	Sight Words First Appearance
4	a, also, am, an, and, be, been, but, can, have, I, of, plays, should, the, think, was
5	always, animals, at, do, food, from, get, good, if, like, never, other, them, to, very, want, with
7	does, don't, important, in, is, it, it's, one, said, this, were, why
8	as, did, not, on, sound
10	asked, big, day, must, run, so, we, you
13	go, much, off, set, started, took, walked, when, who, would
14	made, my, see
17	down, he, here, how, line, still, time
18	make, that
20	because, could, feet, help, him, his, move, over, too
22	after, are, end, near
25	all, came, into, next, stop, they, up
27	thought

Page	Content Words First Appearance
4	actor, leader, lion, manager, narrator, prop man, rabbit, screenwriter, theater
5	dance, music, pig
7	hare, lesson, race, tortoise
8	curtain, gong, stage
10	field, hill, top
13	whistle
14	shell
17	shade
18	path, rocks
22	flag
25	bottom
27	audience, everybody

Check out av2books.com for your animated storytime media enhanced book!

1. Go to av2books.com

2. Enter book code

Y 1 2 2 5 2 3

3. Fuel your imagination online!

www.av2books.com

AV² Storytime Navigation

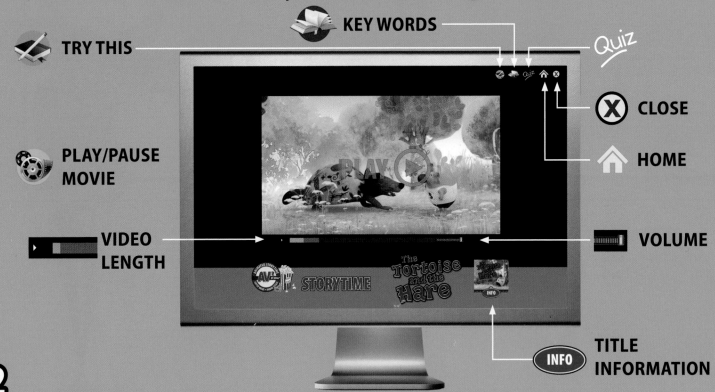

KEY WORDS

TRY THIS

Quiz

X CLOSE

PLAY/PAUSE MOVIE

HOME

VIDEO LENGTH

VOLUME

STORYTIME

The Tortoise and the Hare

INFO

TITLE INFORMATION